First published in the United States, Great Britain, Canada, Australia, and New
Zealand in 2010 by NorthSouth Books Inc., an imprint of NordSüd Verlag AG,
CH-8050 Zürich, Switzerland.
Distributed in the United States by NorthSouth Books Inc., New York 10016.

Library of Congress Cataloging-in-Publication Data is available.
Printed in Latvia, 2018
ISBN: 978-0-7358-2330-3 (trade edition)
3 5 7 9 • 10 8 6 4 2

www.northsouth.com

The Star Child

The Brothers Grimm • illustrated by Bernadette Watts

translated and adapted by J. Alison James

North
South

There was once a little girl named Mathilde who had no mother
or father. She had no home to live in, nor bed to rest on at night.
All she had were the clothes on her back and a piece of bread that
some kind soul had given to her. But she had a loving and courageous
heart, so she set out across the land to see what might happen.

Along her way, she met an old man who was so hungry
that when he saw her bread, he started to tremble.

"Here," Mathilde said kindly. "You have greater need of this
than I do." And she gave him the entire piece.

She went along. After a while, she met a little boy whose ears and cheeks were raw with cold. Mathilde said to him, "Would you like my hat? My head is warm enough for me."

The little boy's eyes opened wide in surprise when he put on the soft hat. "Thank you," he said, and his happiness made her heart grow warm.

Farther along the road, Mathilde came across a young boy with his mother. The boy had only a thin shirt, and his arms were scratched from the wood he carried. Mathilde thought how much warmer and safer he'd be if only he had her coat. So she took it off and offered it to him.

The coat was a little big, but it was so warm that the boy was delighted.

Mathilde went on her way. The sun was starting to go down, and she was a bit hungry and was growing cold. But as she sat under a tree to rest her feet, she thought about the people she had been able to make happy, and that helped.

Soon after she started walking again, she met a child out on the road with tears in her eyes.

"What is wrong?" she asked.

"I have no dress to wear. All I have is this sack. It's so itchy, it keeps me from sleeping."

Mathilde thought about what to do and decided that she could live without her own dress. "Here," she said, "take mine. It is long and soft. It will last a long time."

The girl was so happy she hugged Mathilde like a sister.

Wearing just her shift, Mathilde went into the woods hoping that she would find a place to sleep for the night. She thought perhaps she could curl up beside a warm deer or a family of rabbits.

But there in the woods she met a family so poor, their young child
had nothing to wear but a piece of dirty cloth.

Mathilde thought, "It is night, and I am in the forest.
Nobody will see me undressed if I give this child my shift."

So she pulled it off and gave it to the child with her blessings.
Though it was late and the child was surely tired from walking,
she danced away wearing the new white shift.

At last Mathilde found a clearing where she could rest her head for the night. With her heart full of joy, she looked up at the stars, which seemed unusually bright that night.

Then a miracle happened. Some of the stars loosened their hold on the dark sky and fell. They whirled through the night, showering sparks of light, and rang like bells when they landed at her feet. They had become shining golden coins.

Then the mists between the stars wove themselves together and floated down to form a dress of finest linen, a shawl of lace, and boots as soft and warm as eiderdown.

In this way Mathilde was rewarded for her kindness, and she was able to grow into a happy young woman with enough for herself and more left over so that she could always help a stranger in need.